THE FRANCES TREASURY

Bread and Jam for Frances
A Baby Sister for Frances
A Birthday for Frances
Best Friends for Frances

Four books written by RUSSELL HOBAN
illustrated by LILLIAN HOBAN

BARNES & NOBLE BOOKS
NEW YORK

HarperCollins*Publishers*

for Julia,
who likes to practice
with a string bean
when she can

BREAD AND JAM
FOR FRANCES

by RUSSELL HOBAN
Pictures by LILLIAN HOBAN

HarperCollins*Publishers*

It was breakfast time,
and everyone was at the table.
Father was eating his egg.
Mother was eating her egg.
Gloria was sitting in a high chair and eating her egg too.
Frances was eating bread and jam.
"What a lovely egg!" said Father.
"If there is one thing I am fond of for breakfast,
it is a soft-boiled egg."
"Yes," said Mother, spooning up egg for the baby,
"it is just the thing to start the day off right."
"Ah!" said Gloria, and ate up her egg.
Frances did not eat her egg.
She sang a little song to it.

She sang the song very softly:

I do not like the way you slide,
I do not like your soft inside,
I do not like you lots of ways,
And I could do for many days
Without eggs.

"What did you say, Frances?" asked Father.
"Nothing," said Frances,
spreading jam on another slice of bread.
"Why do you keep eating bread and jam," asked Father,
"when you have a lovely soft-boiled egg?"
"One of the reasons I like bread and jam," said Frances,
"is that it does not slide off your spoon in a funny way."

"Well, of course," said Father,
"not everyone is fond of soft-boiled eggs for breakfast.
But there are other kinds of eggs.
There are sunny-side-up and sunny-side-down eggs."
"Yes," said Frances. "But sunny-side-up eggs
lie on the plate and look up at you in a funny way.
And sunny-side-down eggs just lie on their stomachs and *wait*."
"What about scrambled eggs?" said Father.
"Scrambled eggs fall off the fork
and roll under the table," said Frances.
"I think it is time for you to go to school now,"
said Mother.

Frances picked up her books, her lunch box,
and her skipping rope.
Then she kissed Mother and Father good-bye
and went to the bus stop.

While she waited for the bus she skipped and sang:

Jam on biscuits, jam on toast,
Jam is the thing that I like most.
Jam is sticky, jam is sweet,
Jam is tasty, jam's a treat—
Rasp*berry,* straw*berry,* goose*berry,* I'm *very*
FOND . . . OF . . . JAM!

That evening for dinner Mother cooked
breaded veal cutlets, with string beans and baked potatoes.
"Ah!" said Father. "What is there handsomer on a plate
and tastier to eat than breaded veal cutlet!"
"It *is* a nice dish, isn't it?" said Mother.
"Eat up the string bean, Gloria."
"Oh!" said Gloria, and ate it up.
She had already eaten her dinner of strained beef
and sweet potatoes, but she liked to practice
with a string bean when she could.

"Where do breaded veal cutlets come from?" asked Frances.
"And why are French-cut stringless beans called *string* beans?"
"We can talk about that another time," said Father.
"Now it is time to eat our dinner."
Frances looked at her plate and sang:

> *What do cutlets wear before they're breaded?*
> *Flannel nightgowns? Cowboy boots?*
> *Furry jackets? Sailor suits?*

Then she spread jam on a slice of bread and took a bite.
"She won't try *anything* new," said Mother to Father.
"She just eats bread and jam."
"How do you know what you'll like
if you won't even try anything?" asked Father.
"Well," said Frances,
"there are many different things to eat,
and they taste many different ways.
But when I have bread and jam
I always know what I am getting, and I am always pleased."
"You try new things in your school lunches," said Mother.
"Today I gave you a chicken-salad sandwich."

"There, now!" said Father to Frances. "Wasn't it good?"

"Well," said Frances, "I traded it to Albert."

"For what?" said Father.

"Bread and jam," said Frances.

The next morning at breakfast Father sat down and said,
"Now I call that a pretty sight!
Fresh orange juice and poached eggs on toast.
There's a proper breakfast for you!"
"Thank you for saying so," said Mother.
"Poached eggs on toast *do* have a cheery look, I think."
Frances began to sing a poached-egg song:

> *Poached eggs on toast, why do you shiver*
> *With such a funny little quiver?*

Then she looked down and saw
that she did not have a poached egg.

"I have no poached egg," said Frances.
"I have nothing but orange juice."
"I know," said Mother.
"Why is that?" said Frances.
"Everybody else has a poached egg.
Even Gloria has a poached egg,
and she is nothing but a baby."
"But you do not like eggs," said Mother,
"and that is why I did not poach one for you.
Have some bread and jam if you are hungry."
So Frances ate bread and jam and went to school.

When the bell rang for lunch
Frances sat down next to her friend Albert.
"What do you have today?" said Frances.
"I have a cream cheese-cucumber-and-tomato sandwich
on rye bread," said Albert. "And a pickle to go with it.
And a hard-boiled egg and a little cardboard shaker of salt
to go with that. And a thermos bottle of milk.

And a bunch of grapes and a tangerine.
And a cup custard and a spoon to eat it with.
What do you have?"
Frances opened her lunch. "Bread and jam," she said,
"and milk."
"You're lucky," said Albert. "That's just what you like.
You don't have to trade now."

"That's right," said Frances. "And I had bread and jam
for dinner last night and for breakfast this morning."
"You certainly are lucky," said Albert.
"Yes," said Frances. "I am a very lucky girl, I guess.
But I'll trade you if you *want* to."
"That's all right," said Albert.
"I *like* cream cheese with cucumbers and tomatoes on rye."
Albert took two napkins from his lunch box.
He tucked one napkin under his chin.
He spread the other one on his desk like a tablecloth.
He arranged his lunch neatly on the napkin.
With his spoon he cracked the shell of the hard-boiled egg.
He peeled away the shell and bit off the end of the egg.
He sprinkled salt on the yolk and set the egg down again.
He unscrewed his thermos-bottle cup and filled it with milk.
Then he was ready to eat his lunch.

He took a bite of sandwich, a bite of pickle,
a bite of hard-boiled egg, and a drink of milk.
Then he sprinkled more salt on the egg and went around again.
Albert made the sandwich, the pickle,
the egg, and the milk come out even.

He ate his bunch of grapes and his tangerine.
Then he cleared away the crumpled-up waxed paper,
the eggshell, and the tangerine peel.
He set the cup custard in the middle of the napkin on his desk.
He took up his spoon and ate up all the custard.
Then Albert folded up his napkins and put them away.
He put away his cardboard saltshaker and his spoon.
He screwed the cup on top of his thermos bottle.
He shut his lunch box,
put it back inside his desk, and sighed.
"I like to have a good lunch," said Albert.
Frances ate her bread and jam and drank her milk.

Then she went out to the playground and skipped rope.
She did not skip as fast as she had skipped in the morning,
and she sang:

> *Jam in the morning, jam at noon,*
> *Bread and jam by the light of the moon.*
> *Jam . . . is . . . very . . . nice.*

When Frances got home from school, Mother said,
"I know you like to have a little snack
when you get home from school,
and I have one all ready for you."
"I *do* like snacks!" said Frances, running to the kitchen.
"Here it is," said Mother. "A glass of milk
and some nice bread and jam for you."

"Aren't you worried that maybe I will get sick
and all my teeth will fall out
from eating so much bread and jam?" asked Frances.
"I don't think that will happen for quite a while,"
said Mother. "So eat it all up and enjoy it."
Frances ate up most of her bread and jam,
but she did not eat all of it.
After her snack she went outside to skip rope.

Frances skipped a little more slowly than she had skipped
at noon, and she sang:

Jam for snacks and jam for meals,
I know how a jam jar feels—
FULL . . . OF . . . JAM!

That evening for dinner Mother cooked
spaghetti and meatballs with tomato sauce.
"I am glad to see there will be enough for second helpings,"
said Father.
"Because spaghetti and meatballs is one of my favorite dishes."

"Spaghetti and meatballs is a favorite with everybody,"
said Mother. "Try a little spaghetti, Gloria."
"Um," said Gloria, and tried the spaghetti.
Frances looked down at her plate
and saw that there was no spaghetti and meatballs on it.
There was a slice of bread and a jar of jam.
Frances began to cry.

"My goodness!" said Mother. "Frances is crying!"

"What is the matter?" asked Father.

Frances looked down at her plate and sang a little sad song.
She sang so softly that Mother and Father could scarcely hear her:

> *What I am*
> *Is tired of jam.*

"I want spaghetti and meatballs," said Frances.
"May I have some, please?"

"I had no idea you liked spaghetti and meatballs!"
said Mother.

"How do you know what I'll like if you won't even try me?"
asked Frances, wiping her eyes.
So Mother gave Frances spaghetti and meatballs,
and she ate it all up.

The next day when the bell rang for lunch,
Albert said, "What do you have today?"
"Well," said Frances, laying a paper doily on her desk
and setting a tiny vase of violets in the middle of it,
"let me see." She arranged her lunch on the doily.

"I have a thermos bottle with cream of tomato soup," she said.
"And a lobster-salad sandwich on thin slices of white bread.
I have celery, carrot sticks, and black olives,
and a little cardboard shaker of salt for the celery.
And two plums and a tiny basket of cherries.
And vanilla pudding with chocolate sprinkles
and a spoon to eat it with."
"That's a good lunch," said Albert.
"I think it's nice that there are all different kinds
of lunches and breakfasts and dinners and snacks.
I think eating is nice."
"So do I," said Frances,
and she made the lobster-salad sandwich, the celery,
the carrot sticks, and the olives come out even.

The End

A BABY SISTER
FOR FRANCES

by RUSSELL HOBAN
Pictures by LILLIAN HOBAN

HarperCollinsPublishers

For Barbara Alexandra Dicks,
who often signs her name in lower case
but is, in fact, a capital person

It was a quiet evening.
Father was reading his newspaper.
Mother was feeding Gloria, the new baby.
Frances was sitting under the kitchen sink.
She was singing a little song:

Plinketty, plinketty, plinketty, plink,
Here is the dishrag that's under the sink.
Here are the buckets and brushes and me,
Plinketty, plinketty, plinketty, plee.

She stopped the song and listened.
Nobody said anything.

Frances went to her room and took some gravel
out of the drawer where she had been saving it.
She put the gravel into her empty coffee can
and put the lid back on the can.
Frances marched into the living room
and rattled the gravel in the can.
As she marched she sang a marching song:

Here we go marching, rattley bang!

"Please don't do that, Frances," said Father.
Frances stopped.
"All right," she said.
She went back to the kitchen and sat down under the sink.
Mother came in, carrying Gloria.
"Why are you sitting under the sink?" said Mother.
"I like it here," said Frances. "It's cozy."
"Would you like to help me put Gloria to bed?" said Mother.

"How much allowance does Gloria get?" said Frances.
"She is too little to have an allowance," said Father.
"Only big girls like you get allowances.
Isn't it nice to be a big sister?"
"May I have a penny along with my nickel
now that I am a big sister?" said Frances.
"Yes," said Father. "Now your allowance
will be six cents a week because you are a big sister."
"Thank you," said Frances.
"I know a girl who gets seventeen cents a week.
She gets three nickels and two pennies."
"Well," said Father, "it's time for bed now."
Father picked Frances up from under the sink
and gave her a piggyback ride to bed.

Mother and Father tucked her in and kissed her good night.
"I need my tiny special blanket," said Frances.
Mother gave her the tiny special blanket.
"And I need my tricycle and my sled
and both teddy bears
and my alligator doll," said Frances.
Father brought in the tricycle and the sled
and both teddy bears and the alligator doll.
Mother and Father kissed her good night again
and Frances went to sleep.

In the morning Frances got up and washed
and began to dress for school.
"Is my blue dress ready for me to wear?" said Frances.
"Oh, dear," said Mother, "I was so busy with Gloria
that I did not have time to iron it,
so you'll have to wear the yellow one."
Mother buttoned Frances up the back.
Then she brushed her hair and put a new ribbon in it
and put her breakfast on the table.
"Why did you put sliced bananas on the oatmeal?"
said Frances.
"Did you forget that I like raisins?"
"No, I did not forget," said Mother,
"but you finished up the raisins yesterday
and I have not been out shopping yet."

8

"Well," said Frances, "things are not very good
around here anymore. No clothes to wear.
No raisins for the oatmeal.
I think maybe I'll run away."
"Finish your breakfast," said Mother.
"It is almost time for the school bus."
"What time will dinner be tonight?" said Frances.
"Half past six," said Mother.
"Then I will have plenty of time to run away
after dinner," said Frances,
and she kissed her mother good-bye
and went to school.

After dinner that evening
Frances packed her little knapsack very carefully.
She put in her tiny special blanket and her alligator doll.
She took all of the nickels and pennies
out of her bank, for travel money,
and she took her good luck coin for good luck.
Then she took a box of prunes from the kitchen
and five chocolate sandwich cookies.

"Well," said Frances, "it is time to say good-bye.
I am on my way. Good-bye."
"Where are you running away to?" said Father.
"I think that under the dining-room table is the best place,"
said Frances. "It's cozy,
and the kitchen is near if I run out of cookies."
"That is a good place to run away to," said Mother,
"but I'll miss you."
"I'll miss you too," said Father.
"Well," said Frances, "good-bye," and she ran away.

Father sat down with his newspaper.

Mother took up the sweater she was knitting.

Father put down the newspaper.

"You know," he said, "it is not the same house without Frances."

"That is just *exactly* what I was thinking," said Mother.

"The place seems lonesome and empty without her."

Frances sat under the dining-room table and ate her prunes.

"Even Gloria," said Mother, "as small as she is,
can feel the difference."

"I can hear her crying a little right now," said Father.

"Well," said Mother, "a girl looks up to an older sister.
You know that."

Father picked up his newspaper.
Then he put it down again.
"I miss the songs that Frances used to sing," he said.
"I was *so* fond of those little songs," said Mother.
"Do you remember the one about the tomato?
'What does the tomato say, early in the dawn?'" sang Mother.
"'Time to be all red again, now that night is gone,'" sang Father.
"Yes," he said, "that is a good one, but my favorite

has always been: 'When the wasps and the bumblebees have a party, nobody comes that can't buzz. . . .'"
"Well," said Mother, "we shall just have to get used to a quiet house now."

Frances ate three of the sandwich cookies
and put the other two aside for later.
She began to sing:

I am poor and hungry here, eating prunes and rice.
Living all alone is not really very nice.

She had no rice, but chocolate sandwich cookies
did not sound right for the song.

"I can almost hear her now," said Father,
humming the tune that Frances had just sung.
"She has a charming voice."
"It is just not a *family* without Frances," said Mother.
"Babies are very nice. Goodness knows I *like* babies,
but a baby is not a family."
"Isn't that a fact!" said Father.
"A family is *everybody all together.*"

"Remember," said Mother, "how I used to say,
'Think how lucky the new baby will be
to have a sister like Frances'?"
"I remember that very well," said Father,
"and I hope that Gloria turns out
to be as clever and good as Frances."
"With a big sister like Frances to help her along,
she ought to turn out just fine," said Mother.
"I'd like to hear from Frances," said Father,
"just to know how she is getting along in her new place."
"I'd like to hear from Frances too," said Mother,
"and I'm not sure the sleeves are right
on this sweater I'm knitting for her."

"Hello," called Frances from the dining room.
"I am calling on the telephone. Hello, hello,
this is me. Is that you?"

"Hello," said Mother. "This is us. How are you?"
"I am fine," said Frances. "This is a nice place,
but you miss your family when you're away. How are you?"
"We are all well," said Father, "but we miss you too."
"I will be home soon," said Frances, and she hung up.

"She said that she will be home soon," said Father.
"That is good news indeed," said Mother.
"I think I'll bake a cake."
Frances put on her knapsack and sang
a little traveling song:

> *Big sisters really have to stay*
> *At home, not travel far away,*
> *Because everybody misses them*
> *And wants to hug-and-kisses them.*

"I'm not sure about that last rhyme," said Frances
as she arrived in the living room
and took off her knapsack.
"That's a good enough rhyme," said Father.
"I like it fine," said Mother,
and they both hugged and kissed her.

"What kind of cake are you baking?" said Frances to Mother.
"Chocolate," said Mother.
"It's too bad that Gloria's too little to have some,"
said Frances, "but when she's a big girl like me,
she can have chocolate cake too."
"Oh, yes," said Mother, "you may be sure that
there will always be plenty of chocolate cake around here."

The End

A BIRTHDAY
FOR FRANCES

by RUSSELL HOBAN

Pictures by LILLIAN HOBAN

HarperCollinsPublishers

for Lynn Klotz
    who would certainly give
    her little sister a Chompo Bar
    if she had a little sister

It was the day before
Frances's little sister Gloria's birthday.
Mother and Gloria were sitting at the kitchen table,
making place cards for the party.
Frances was in the broom closet, singing:

Happy Thursday to you,
Happy Thursday to you,
Happy Thursday, dear Alice,
Happy Thursday to you.

"Who is Alice?" asked Mother.
"Alice is somebody that nobody can see,"
said Frances. "And that is why
she does not have a birthday. So I am singing
Happy Thursday to her."

"Today is Friday," said Mother.
"It is Thursday for Alice," said Frances.
"Alice will not have h-r-n-d,
and she will not have g-k-l-s.
But we are singing together."
"What are h-r-n-d and g-k-l-s?" asked Mother.
"Cake and candy. I thought you could spell,"
said Frances.
"I am sure that Alice will have
cake and candy on her birthday," said Mother.
"But Alice does not have a birthday,"
said Frances.

"Yes, she does," said Mother.
"Even if nobody can see her,
Alice has one birthday every year, and so do you.
Your birthday is two months from now.
Then you will be the birthday girl.
But tomorrow is Gloria's birthday,
and she will be the birthday girl."
"That is how it is, Alice," said Frances.
"Your birthday is always the one that is not now."

"Frances," said Mother, "wouldn't you and Alice
like to come out of the broom closet
and help us make place cards for the party?"
Frances came to the table
and sat down and picked up a crayon.
"What are you putting on the place cards?"
she asked.
"Pretty flowers," said Gloria.
"Rainbows and happy trees."
Frances began to draw on a place card,
and as she drew she sang:

A rainbow and a happy tree
Are not for Alice or for me.
I will draw three-legged cats.
And caterpillars with ugly hats.

Frances stopped singing. "I'm telling," she said.
"Telling what?" said Mother.
"Gloria kicked me under the table,"
said Frances.
"Mean Frances," said Gloria.

"Gloria is mean," said Frances.
"She hid my sand pail and my shovel,
and I never got them back."
"That was last year," said Mother.
"When Gloria is mean, it was always last year,"
said Frances. "But me and Alice know s-m-f-o."

"What is s-m-f-o?" asked Mother.

"Better," said Frances. "Good-bye.

I will be out of town visiting Alice for two weeks,

and I will be back for dinner."

She went to the broom closet

and took out her favorite broom.

"Let's go, Champ," she said. "I'm ready to ride."

Frances climbed onto the broom

and galloped out of the kitchen

while Mother and Gloria finished the place cards.

Then Gloria went out to play

while Mother wrapped her presents in the living room.

Frances was riding back and forth

on her broom on the porch, and as she rode

she sang a song for Alice:

> *Everybody makes a fuss*
> *For birthday girls who are not us.*
> *Girls who take your pail away*
> *Eat cake and q-p-m all day.*

"Is q-p-m ice cream?" Mother asked Frances

through the window.

"Yes," said Frances. She climbed up
on one of the porch rocking chairs
and looked through the window
at the boxes Mother was wrapping.
"What is Gloria getting from you and from Father
for her birthday?" asked Frances.

"A paintbox and a tea set and a plush pig,"
said Mother.
"I am not going to give Gloria any present,"
said Frances.
"That is all right," said Mother,
and Frances began to cry.
"What is the matter?" said Mother.
"Why are you crying?"
"Everybody is giving Gloria a present but me,"
said Frances.

"Would you like to give Gloria a present?"
said Mother.
"Yes," said Frances. "If I had
my next two allowances, I would have
a nickel and two pennies and another
nickel and two pennies, and I could buy
a Chompo Bar and four balls of bubble gum for Gloria."
"I think it is very nice of you
to want to give Gloria a birthday present,"
said Mother, and she gave Frances
her next two allowances.
That evening Father took Frances
to the candy store to buy a Chompo Bar
and four balls of bubble gum for Gloria.

As they walked home Frances said to Father,
"Are you sure that it is all right
for Gloria to have a whole Chompo Bar?
Maybe she is too young for that kind of candy.
Maybe it will make her sick."
"Well," said Father, "I do not think
it would be good for Gloria to eat Chompo Bars
every day. But tomorrow is her birthday,
and I think it will be
all right for her to eat one."

Frances thought about Gloria and the Chompo Bar,
and while she thought she put
two of the bubble-gum balls into her mouth
without noticing it.
She chewed the bubble gum
and squeezed the Chompo Bar a little.

"Chompo Bars have a soft nougat part inside,"
said Frances, "and there is a chewy caramel part
around that, and the outside is chocolate with nuts.
Probably Gloria could not eat more than half of one."
"Gloria loves sweets," said Father,
"and I am sure that she can eat the whole Chompo Bar.
That is why it is such a good present for her,
and you were very nice to think of it."
"Yes," said Frances,
"and I spent two allowances on Gloria."
While Frances was thinking about the two allowances
she put the other two balls of bubble gum
into her mouth and chewed them,
and she squeezed the Chompo Bar and sang:

> *Chompo Bars are nice to get.*
> *Chompo Bars taste better yet*
> *When they're someone else's.*

"You would not eat Gloria's Chompo Bar,
would you?" said Father.
"It is not Gloria's yet," said Frances.
"I can hardly understand what you are saying,"
said Father. "Is there something in your mouth?"

"I think maybe there is bubble gum,"
said Frances, "but I don't remember
how it got there."
"Maybe I should take care of the Chompo Bar
until you are ready to give it to Gloria,"
said Father.
"All right," said Frances,
and she gave the Chompo Bar to Father
to take care of.

The next day was Gloria's birthday,
and the party was that afternoon.
The cake was ready; the table was all set;
and Mother was making hot chocolate.
There were little baskets of gum drops
and chocolate-covered peanuts for everybody.
There were place cards and party poppers
for Mother and Father, for Frances and Gloria,
for Gloria's friend Ida,
and for Frances's friend Albert.

Albert was the first friend to arrive,
and he and Frances sat down in the living room
while they were waiting for Ida.
"What are you giving Gloria?"
Frances asked Albert.
"A little tiny truck in a little tiny box,"
said Albert.

"The kind that costs fifty cents?" asked Frances.

"That's right," said Albert.

"But my mother gave me the money for it."

"I am thinking of giving Gloria a Chompo Bar,"
said Frances. "But I am not sure.
I might and I might not. I had to spend
almost two whole allowances on it."

"That's how it is when it's your own sister,"
said Albert. "I had to spend
my allowance money on my little sister
when she had a birthday.
I gave her a yo-yo. But she is not
high enough off the ground for a yo-yo.
So I get to use it."

"Little sisters are not much r-v-s-m,"
said Frances.

"Good?" said Albert.

"That's right," said Frances.

"No, they are not," said Albert.

"They can't catch. They can't throw.
When you play hide-and-seek, they always hide
in places where part of them is sticking out."

"They take your sand pail and your shovel too,"
said Frances. "They pull the button eyes
off dolls that have button eyes.
They break your crayons so there are no long ones
left in the box. They put water in your mud pies
when you don't want them to.
I don't think many of them deserve a Chompo Bar."

"You can't use a Chompo Bar over and over
like a yo-yo," said Albert. "One time and it's gone.
You should at least get part of it."
"That's right," said Frances.
"Here is Ida now," said Mother,
"and the party can begin."

"When are the presents?" said Gloria
as they all sat down at the places
where their place cards were.
"First," said Father, "your mother
will bring out the cake, and I will light the candles.
Then we will all sing 'Happy Birthday to You.'
Then you make a wish and blow out all the candles.
Then you get your presents."
"I know what to wish," said Gloria.

"Don't tell it," said Ida.
"It won't come true if you do," said Albert.
"Here comes the cake," said Mother.
She put it on the table,
and Father lit the candles.
Then everybody sang "Happy Birthday to You."
Frances did not sing the words
that the others were singing.
Very softly, so that nobody could hear her,
she sang:

> *Happy Chompo to me*
> *Is how it ought to be—*
> *Happy Chompo to Frances,*
> *Happy Chompo to me.*

"Now," said Mother to Gloria, "make your wish
and blow out the candles."
"I want to tell my wish," said Gloria.
"No, no!" said Mother and Father
and Frances and Albert and Ida.
"Just say it inside your head
and blow out the candles," said Albert.
Gloria said her wish inside her head
and blew out all the candles at once.
"Hooray!" said everybody.

"Now your wish will come true," said Mother.

"This is what I wished," said Gloria:

"I wished that Frances would be nice
and not be mad at me because I hid her sand pail
and shovel last year. And I am sorry,
and I will be nice."

"She told," said Ida. "Now her wish won't come true."

"I think it will come true," said Mother,
"because it is a special kind of good wish
that can make itself come true."

"Well," said Frances to Gloria,
"I think your wish will come true too.
And I have a present for you,
and I owe you four balls of bubble gum."
"Now is it time for the presents?" said Gloria.
"Yes," said Father.
Father and Mother gave Gloria the paintbox
and the tea set and the plush pig.
Albert gave her the little tiny truck.
Ida gave her a little china baby doll.
Frances had wrapped the Chompo Bar
in pretty paper and tied it with a ribbon,
and now she got ready to give it to Gloria.

"What is it?" asked Gloria.
"It is something good to eat," said Frances,
"and I will give it to you in a minute.
But first I will sing 'Happy Birthday to You,'
because I did not really sing it before.
Happy birthday to you," sang Frances,
and she squeezed the Chompo Bar.
"Happy birthday to you." Then she stopped
and rested a little.
"You can have a bite when I get it," said Gloria.

Frances took a deep breath and finished the song,
"Happy birthday, dear Gloria, happy birthday to you.
Here," said Frances. She squeezed the Chompo Bar
one last time and gave it to Gloria.
"You can eat it all, because
you are the birthday girl," said Frances.
"Thank you," said Gloria
as she quickly unwrapped the Chompo Bar.
"This is a good present." And she ate it all,
because she was the birthday girl.

BEST FRIENDS
FOR FRANCES

by Russell Hoban

Pictures by Lillian Hoban

![HarperCollins logo] HarperCollinsPublishers

For Frances's friends everywhere

It was a pleasant summer morning,
so Frances took her bat and her ball
and some chocolate sandwich cookies and went outside.
"Will you play ball with me?" Frances's little sister
Gloria called to her as she was leaving.
"No," said Frances. "You are too little."
Gloria sat down on the back steps and cried.
Frances walked over to her friend Albert's house,
singing a little song:

> *Sisters that are much too small*
> *To throw or catch or bat a ball*
> *Are really not much good at all,*
> *Except for crying.*

When Frances got to Albert's house,
he was just coming out, and he was carrying
a large, heavy-looking brown paper bag.
"Let's play baseball," said Frances.
"I can't," said Albert. "Today is my wandering day."
"Where do you wander?" said Frances.
"I don't know," said Albert. "I just go around
until I get hungry, and then I eat my lunch."
"That looks like a big lunch," said Frances.
"It's nothing much," said Albert. "Four or five

sandwiches and some apples and bananas
and two packages of cupcakes
 and a quart of chocolate milk."
"Can I wander with you?" asked Frances.
"I only have one lunch," said Albert.
"I'll bring my own," said Frances.
"I'll run home and get it right away."
"No," said Albert. "I think I better go by myself.
The things I do on my wandering days
aren't things you can do."

"Like what?" said Frances.

"Catching snakes," said Albert. "Throwing stones at telephone poles. A little frog work maybe. Walking on fences. Whistling with grass blades. Looking for crow feathers."

"I can do all that," said Frances, "except for the frog work and the snakes."

"That's what I mean," said Albert. "I'd have to ruin the whole day, showing you how. I'll see you tomorrow."

Then Albert went off to wander, and Frances walked slowly home with her bat and ball, singing:

> *Fat boys that eat too much lunch*
> *Can't do a thing but munch and crunch*
> *And play with snakes and frogs.*

When Frances got home, Gloria said, "Will you play ball with me now?"

"You can't bat and you can't catch," said Frances, "and you can't throw either."

"I can if you stand close," said Gloria.

"All right," said Frances, and she played ball with Gloria.

The next morning when Frances went to Albert's house,
Albert was playing ball with his friend Harold.

"Can I play?" asked Frances.

"She's not much good," said Harold to Albert,
"and besides, this is a no-girls game."

"Can't I play?" said Frances to Albert.

"Well, it *is* a no-girls game," said Albert.

"All right," said Frances. "Then I will go home
and play a no-boys game with my sister Gloria,
Mr. Fat Albert. So ha, ha, ha."
Frances walked home, and as she walked she sang:

Boys to throw and catch and bat
Are all the friends that Mr. Fat
Albert will have from now on.
He will not have me.

When Frances got home, Gloria said,
"How did you play so fast that you are home so soon?"
"It was a fast game," said Frances.
"You're lucky that you have a friend to play with,"
said Gloria. "I wish I had a friend."

"I thought Ida was your friend," said Frances.

"Ida is away at camp," said Gloria,

"and when she is here she only wants to play

dolls or tea party. She never wants

to catch frogs or play ball."

"Can you catch frogs?" asked Frances.

"I use Father's old hat," said Gloria.

"Shall I show you how?"

"Later," said Frances. "Do you want to play ball?"

"All right," said Gloria.

"If any boys come, they can't play," said Frances,

"and I think I will be your friend now."

"How can a sister be a friend?" said Gloria.

"You'll see," said Frances.

"For frogs and ball *and* tea parties and dolls?"

said Gloria.

"Yes," said Frances.

"And will you show me how to print my name?"
said Gloria. "And tell me what the letters and numbers
say when I make letters and numbers?"
"Yes," said Frances.
"Then you will be my best friend," said Gloria.
"Will it be just today, or longer?"
"Longer," said Frances. "And today we are going to do
something big, with no boys."
"What?" said Gloria.
"We will have an outing," said Frances,
"and there will be a picnic and songs
and games and prizes."
Mother helped Frances and Gloria get everything ready
and packed in Frances's wagon.

Then Frances and Gloria went off to the outing.
In the wagon was a picnic lunch in a hamper.
There were also two burlap sacks for the sack race,
an egg for the egg toss, and a jar with two frogs in it
that Gloria had caught for the frog-jumping contest.
And there were balloons and lollipops for prizes.
Frances had made a sign to carry on the outing too.
It said:

BEST FRIENDS

OUTING

NO BOYS

Frances and Gloria held the sign high
as they passed Albert's house, and Frances sang:

When best friends have an outing,
There are jolly times in store.
There are games and there are prizes,
There is also something more.
There is something in a hamper
That is very good to eat.
When best friends have an outing,
It's a very special treat,
With no boys.

"What is in that hamper?" asked Albert
as he came running out of his house.
"I don't know," said Frances. "Nothing much.
Hard-boiled eggs and whole fresh tomatoes.
Carrot and celery sticks. There are some
cream cheese-and-chives sandwiches, I think,
and cream cheese-and-jelly sandwiches too,
and salami-and-egg and pepper-and-egg sandwiches.
Cole slaw and potato chips, of course.
Ice-cold root beer packed in ice,
and watermelon and strawberries and cream for dessert.

And there are other things I forget,
like black and green olives and pickles and Popsicles
and probably some pretzels and things like that.
And there are salt and pepper shakers and napkins
and a checked tablecloth,
which is the way girls do it."
"Could I come along on the eating?" said Albert.
"You mean outing," said Frances.
"Outing, I mean," said Albert. "Could I come along?
That wagon looks very heavy to pull,
and you will probably get all tired out unless I help you."
"I don't know," said Frances.
"You can see from the sign that this is a no-boys outing
and it is only for best friends."
"What good is an outing without boys?" said Albert.
"It is just as good as a ball game without girls,"
said Frances, "and maybe a whole lot better."
"Can't I be a best friend?" asked Albert.
"I don't think it is the kind of thing you can do,"
said Frances, "and it would ruin my whole day
to have to explain it to you."

"I can do it," said Gloria.

"I can be a best friend, and I can catch frogs too."

"I can catch frogs *and* snakes," said Albert.

"Let him be a best friend," said Gloria,

"and he can show me how to catch snakes."

"I'll get my snake pillowcase right now," said Albert.

"Well, I'm not sure," said Frances. "Maybe you'll be best friends when it is goodies-in-the-hamper time, but how about when it is no-girls-baseball time?"

"When we are best friends, there won't be
any no-girls baseball," said Albert.
"All right," said Frances, and she crossed out
the NO BOYS on the sign.
Then they started off again. Albert pulled the wagon
to the outing place while Frances and Gloria
walked ahead with the sign.

The outing place was at the maple tree on the hill
by the pond. Everybody had a good time there.
First, Albert caught a snake for Gloria,
and then they played games.
Gloria won the sack race, Frances won the egg toss,
and Albert won the frog-jumping contest
with a fresh frog he caught right there at the pond.
So everybody won a prize. Then Frances
made up a party song, and everybody sang it:

When the wasps and the bumblebees have a party,
Nobody comes that can't buzz.
When the chicks and the ducklings have an outing,
Everyone has to wear fuzz.
When the frog and the snake
Have their yearly clambake,
There's plenty of wiggling and hopping.
They splash in the pond
And the marshes beyond,
And everyone has to get sopping.

"And at the Best Friends Outing," said Albert,
"everyone has to eat, don't they?"
"Yes," said Frances and Gloria, and they opened the hamper.
"Maybe we packed too much," said Frances.
"I'm not sure we can eat it all."
"That is what best friends are for," said Albert
as he quickly spread the tablecloth.
"I will help you finish it all."

That is what Albert did, and when the picnic was over, the hamper was not heavy at all.

"I call that a good outing," said Albert.
And he gave Frances and Gloria a ride in the wagon
while he pulled it all the way home.

The next morning Albert came over
with a bunch of daisies for Frances.
"What are the daisies for?" said Frances.
"Well," said Albert, "we are best friends now,
and I am a boy. So that makes me your best boyfriend,
and that is why I brought you the daisies."
"Thank you," said Frances.
Then Gloria sat down on the steps and cried.
"Why are you crying?" said Frances.

"Because now you have Albert to be your best boyfriend and bring you flowers and play ball with," said Gloria, "and you won't be my best friend anymore."

"Yes, I will," said Frances. "And besides, I am not sure that I am going to let Albert be my boyfriend."

"Then let him be mine," said Gloria.

"Not so fast," said Frances. "It was only yesterday that you got to be big enough to play baseball. But I will give you half the daisies Albert gave me."

So Frances gave Gloria half the daisies, and Gloria stopped crying.

Then Harold came over, and everybody played baseball—Gloria too.